WHITE SAND BLUES

VICKI DELANY

ORCA BOOK PUBLISHERS

Library and Archives Canada Cataloguing in Publication

Delany, Vicki, 1951-, author
White sand blues / Vicki Delany.
(Rapid reads)

Issued also in electronic formats.
ISBN 978-1-4598-1535-3 (softcover).—ISBN 978-1-4598-1536-0 (pdf).—
ISBN 978-1-4598-1537-7 (epub)

I. Title. II. Series: Rapid reads
PS8557.E4239W44 2017   C813´.6   C2017-900860-9   C2017-900861-7

First published in the United States, 2017
Library of Congress Control Number: 2017932516

Summary: Paramedic Ashley Grant finds herself in the
middle of a murder investigation while in the Victoria and
Albert Islands in this work of crime fiction. (RL 3.0)

*Orca Book Publishers is dedicated to preserving the environment and has
printed this book on Forest Stewardship Council® certified paper.*

Orca Book Publishers gratefully acknowledges the support for
its publishing programs provided by the following agencies:
the Government of Canada through the Canada Book Fund and the
Canada Council for the Arts, and the Province of British Columbia
through the BC Arts Council and the Book Publishing Tax Credit.

Design by Jenn Playford
Cover photography by iStock.com

ORCA BOOK PUBLISHERS
www.orcabook.com

Printed and bound in Canada.

20   19   18   17   •   4   3   2   1

To Alex, for introducing me to "her" islands

ONE

"YOU WANT ME TO DO WHAT?"

"Start work. Now. We have to get him. No one else is going to." Simon bent over. He began unlacing his boots.

He was wearing black steel-toed work boots. I had on sandals with two-inch heels and thin straps. This was the first time I'd worn them. They'd set me back two hundred bucks I could ill afford. I glanced around. I hoped to see someone, anyone, ready to help.

Curious faces stared back at me. Some of the faces were black or brown.

Most were shiny white. More than a few were a hideous shade of pink. Only Simon and I and the hotel staff were wearing street clothes. Everyone else wore some sort of beach attire. One guy held a sweating glass full of slices of tropical fruit and a colorful umbrella. Cameras and cell phones were lifted. If anyone told me to smile, I'd smack them.

I looked out to sea. I hoped to see a rescue boat heading to my, well, rescue.

No such luck. The water, at least, was calm.

"Ashley," Simon said. I couldn't see his eyes behind his sunglasses, but his jaw was tense. "This is the job. Can you do it or not? If not, there's a flight to Miami leaving at six. I can tell Gord you changed your mind."

That sounded tempting, but I took a deep breath. "Let's do it." I hoped I sounded like a firefighter I'd once heard as he led his men into a burning building. They rescued two children and a cat that day.

My plane had landed on Grand Victoria Island less than an hour earlier. I'd been surprised to see that my new boss had sent an ambulance to meet me. I'd been even more surprised when a call came over the radio and the driver said we were to answer it.

I kicked off my sandals.

I couldn't do much about the sundress. It also had set me back a pretty penny. I'd wanted to start my new life looking like a million bucks. Confident, in control. Dressed for success.

No one had suggested I'd be better in a uniform or hospital scrubs.

Simon didn't look back to see if I followed. He waded into the surf.

I prefer to stay out of the water whenever possible. When I took this job I forgot that an island is surrounded by water. I took a deep breath and followed Simon. The sand beneath my feet was soft and deep. The water was clear. Tiny fish darted around my freshly painted toes.

I kept an eye out for sharks. No fins broke the surface of the sea. No ominous music played. Perhaps these fish were too small for sharks to concern themselves with. I hoped there was no blood. Didn't blood attract sharks?

The sharks aren't the only reason I hate the ocean. There's the seaweed too. *Nothing cleaner*, my dad used to say when we vacationed on a lake in Ontario or the ocean in Nova Scotia. That did nothing to allay my fears. To me the long tendrils seemed like those of a sea monster, reaching out, eager to drag me into the dark depths. They still did.

I squeaked and tried to dodge a dangerous length of seaweed. My toe connected with a submerged rock. I felt a stabbing pain in my right foot. I yelped, jumped and started to fall forward into the water. My arms waved wildly as I fought to keep my footing. I was in no danger of drowning. The water was about fifteen centimeters deep at this point. I spat out salty water and fine grains of sand. As I stumbled to stand, I tried to regain a shred of dignity.

Simon had turned around. He glared at me over the rims of his sunglasses. I could read his mind—*hiring this one was a big mistake.*

I gave him what I hoped was a confident grin and lumbered upright. I dug my bare toes into the sand to steady myself. "Coming," I called.

The bottom of the sea sloped gently. They weren't very far out, so we didn't have to swim. A man waited for us. The water came up to his waist. He was tanned a nut brown and wore a blue T-shirt and shorts. I guessed he was a hotel employee.

The dead man bobbed gently on the surface.

Simon grunted greetings. He—the living man, that is—nodded, his face solemn.

My three-hundred-dollar linen dress with lace edging was being ruined by salt water. My two-hundred-dollar sandals were probably being pinched by a beach urchin with excellent taste. But my training took over as soon as we reached the body. He was lying faceup, staring into the sky. His face was blue, from death and immersion in the water. No doubt he'd been flipped over by the hotel employee.

Simon grabbed the dead man's collar. I put my fingers to the neck. I felt for a pulse. Nothing. I glanced at Simon and shook my head. The dead man was white, in his sixties maybe. Belly like a nine-months-pregnant woman. His thick hair was so jet black that it had to have been dyed. His fingers were long, his nails manicured. A fat gold band encircled the third finger of his left hand. A ring with a big red stone decorated the pinky of his right. His stomach hung over a baggy, knee-length bathing suit. His feet were bare. He hadn't been in the water for too long. Sea creatures hadn't had time to begin making a meal out of his tender bits.

I led the way back to shore. Simon and the hotel employee followed. The body bobbed between them. I wondered where the police rescue boat was. Simon asked the man helping us, Mark, how his son was getting on in school.

"Very well," Mark said. "Thank you for asking."

"This is the Club Louisa," Simon said to me. "One of the best hotels on the island. And on Grand Victoria, best means expensive."

"You got that right," Mark said with a laugh.

We'd parked the ambulance on the lush emerald grass of the hotel grounds. That was as close as we could get to the water without getting the wheels trapped in sand. We'd left the gurney at the edge of the water. The men laid their burden onto it. Mark lifted the front and Simon the rear. We didn't stop to put on boots and shoes before we walked up the beach. The onlookers stood quietly and respectfully. One pink-chested guy held his baseball cap over his heart. A woman crossed herself. I hurried ahead to open the ambulance doors. The crowd of onlookers closed in behind us. More pictures were snapped. I tried to ignore them. A woman waited for us by the ambulance. She was well dressed in a khaki skirt cut at the knee. Her blue shirt had the hotel's yellow sun logo over her breast.

She stepped forward and glanced down at the man on the gurney. He looked past us into the expanse of brilliant-blue sky. I've seen that look often enough that it doesn't bother me. Not anymore.

"Recognize him, Elaine?" Simon asked.

"I think so." Her accent was upper-crust British. "One of ours, I fear."

"I'm sure the police will be around to talk to you about it later," Simon said. His rolling Caribbean accent was soft and gentle.

"Julian! No! Julian." A woman came running up the beach, struggling in the deep sand. Spectators stepped out of her path. A gorgeous sapphire-blue beach gown dotted with gold beads streamed behind her. She wore sexy, barely there gold sandals and a large-brimmed straw hat with a gold scarf wrapped around it. I guessed her to be in her midforties. Following her was a younger woman in a pink-and-white bikini and large sunglasses. Her hair was pulled back into a high ponytail. The older woman took one look at the staring blank face on the gurney and moaned. She crumpled to the ground in a delicate heap.

"Ashley, look after her," Simon said. "She'd better come with us. Let's get outa here."

I crouched beside the woman. Her eyelids fluttered and then opened. "Julian?" she whispered.

"Let me help you." I put one arm around her shoulders and guided her to sit. Her eyes were dark, almost black. Her lips were painted a soft pink, and the studs in her seashell ears appeared to be genuine diamonds. She blinked and touched my chest lightly. Her long nails were painted to match her lipstick. The sun caught the diamond on her finger. The light it threw back was so strong, it could be used to send signals into space.

I helped her to her feet. She swayed slightly, and I kept a grip on her arm.

"Do you know this gentleman?" Simon asked.

"My...my husband. Julian."

"You can come with us. Ashley, you go in the back. Mrs....uh...?"

"Hunt. Christina Hunt."

"The widow Hunt," a sharp voice said.

We all turned. The younger woman who'd followed Mrs. Hunt spoke. "It didn't take long for you to get what you wanted, did it, Christina? The sad, tragic widow. The *rich*, sad, tragic widow."

"Sally, my poor sweet thing," Christina murmured. "You don't know what you're saying." She shook me off. She stretched out her arms. She took a step toward the girl as if to give her a hug.

Sally's body stiffened. "You killed him, Christina. I know it. And I intend to prove it."

"You're overcome by grief, my dear." Christina glanced around. The crowd of spectators was growing, pressing closer. Murmurs began at the word *killed*.

"Sort it out later," Simon said. We loaded the late Mr. Hunt into the ambulance. "Get in," he ordered me.

I was the medic. Simon was my driver. But I was the new one here. I turned, ready to obey.

"Hey, Ashley," Sally said. "How's things?"

TWO

WE LEFT THE BEACH with Christina and the body of her late husband. The hotel manager said she'd call a cab for Sally.

Mark had run down to the water. He'd returned proudly bearing Simon's boots. There was no sign of my expensive sandals.

I studied my formerly lovely linen dress, soaked with salt water, full of sand. It hadn't been a very practical choice anyway for a long plane trip.

Note to self: Don't waste money trying to impress the locals.

I sat in the back of the ambulance with the late Julian Hunt. Through the small windows in the doors I glimpsed tall palm trees, low buildings and a blue sky. The trip took no more than five minutes. I hadn't realized how small this island was until I saw it from the air.

As soon as we got to the hospital, I jumped out. I opened the passenger door for Mrs. Hunt. She sobbed quietly as I took her arm. "Are you…uh…on vacation?" I asked. Stupid question, considering the beach dress.

"I thought a nice relaxing holiday would do Julian good. He's been working so hard lately. He didn't want to take the time off. I insisted. This is all my fault!" Her eyes were red, her mascara a black smudge.

"I'll be right back to help you," I said to Simon. "Let me get Mrs. Hunt inside."

We walked through the swinging doors into the hospital. The reception area was bright and clean.

"Where are you from?" I wanted to keep her talking.

"Picton, Ontario," she said.

"Really? Me too." I hadn't recognized Sally at first. Not until she said my name. Sally Hunt. I'd gone to school with her. We hadn't been friends, but we'd been in many of the same classes, and we had both been on the baseball team. I remembered seeing Sally's parents at school sports events. Her mother had been a mom like all the others. Not this pretty weeping woman.

I found Mrs. Hunt a seat. I was back outside helping Simon unload the gurney when a cab pulled up. Sally leaped out, still wearing her bathing suit. I was glad I'd had the foresight to pull a sheet over her father's face. Simon and I wheeled the gurney into the hospital. Sally followed.

A nurse with a bosom like the prow of an old sailing ship waited for us.

She turned without a word and led the way through a set of doors.

Sally and Christina tried to follow. The nurse lifted a hand. "No entry."

"My husband," Christina protested.

"No entry. Sit down. I said, *sit down*. Someone will be with you shortly."

The two women did as they were told. The doors swung shut behind us.

The nurse held out her hand to me. "You must be the new medic. Welcome. I'm Lucy." Her accent spoke of the backstreets of Glasgow.

We handed over the body of Mr. Hunt to the morgue staff. Simon told me I could go outside and catch some air while he finished the paperwork. "Only because it's your first time here. From now on, you do your own paperwork."

"Better not walk about like that." The morgue assistant pointed to my feet.

It's never a good idea to wander a hospital in one's bare feet.

The assistant rummaged in a locker and pulled out a pair of pink flip-flops. They were chewed around the edges. I hoped the chewing had been done by a playful dog. I slipped them on. Not too dreadfully big.

Christina watched me walk back through the waiting room. Outside, Sally had taken a seat on a patch of weedy grass in the shade of the ambulance. I hadn't even had time to notice how hot it was. The sun beat down on the pavement so hard it made the air above shimmer and shake. Palm trees lined the hospital driveway, not moving in the still, humid air.

Sally slowly got to her feet. Her eyes were dry. "Ashley. Nice to see you."

"I wish it could have been under better circumstances."

Her eyes ran down my body, taking in the ruined dress, the cheap flip-flops. I'd arranged my hair that morning into a neat French braid. Now it hung around my face in salty strands. My lip gloss had been chewed off somewhere out at sea.

"She killed him," Sally said. She pointed with her chin toward the door to the hospital.

"Do you mean your stepmother? That's a heck of a strong accusation."

"Don't call her that. She's my father's wife. She's no relation of mine."

"I'm sure it was an accident."

Sally snorted. "She's been planning it for a long time."

The doors opened, and Simon emerged with the empty gurney. "Your stepmother," he said as Sally growled, "is with your father now. You can go in. I'm sorry for your loss. Ashley, let's go."

"Look," Sally said. "We can't talk here." Hospital staff were coming and going. No one paid us any attention. "Where are you staying?"

"I don't know," I said.

"You don't know?"

I shrugged. "I just got here."

Simon climbed into the driver's seat and switched the engine on. He tapped the horn. I had little doubt he'd leave without me if I didn't hurry up. "I gotta go, Sally. Nice seeing you."

"You know where we're staying. Call me later."

"I don't—"

"I don't have anyone else. No one I can trust. She'll do everything she can to cover it up. I *need* you, Ashley." The look on her face was a combination of emotions. Grief, anger, hate. I hesitated. I'd only just arrived on the island. I wanted time to settle in, get to know people and find my way around.

But the sadness in her eyes had me saying, "Tonight. I'll call you tonight."

I jumped into the ambulance. Simon drove away.

THREE

MY HOTEL WASN'T AS NICE as the Club Louisa. But it came close. The buildings were such a brilliant white, it hurt my eyes to look at them. They were surrounded by thick, green lawns. Masses of purple and white flowers lined the neat walkways. The blue ocean sparkled in the distance. Two sailboats leisurely drifted past.

The wide French doors on the main building opened, and a woman came out. "Welcome to the Ocean Breeze Hotel, Ms. Grant." Her smile was wide and her eyes friendly.

I glanced over my shoulder at Simon. "Home sweet home," he said.

"Wow." I got out of the ambulance.

Simon got my bags out of the back and put them on the driveway. "You have the day off tomorrow to get yourself settled. I'm the regular day-shift driver. I'll pick you up at seven Wednesday morning for your first shift. You'll meet Gord, our boss, then and do all the paperwork. Be on time. Gord expects everyone to be at work on time."

The woman laughed. "Foreigners and their strange ways."

"You need to get yourself a local plan for your phone," Simon said. "You'll be notified if the ambulance is busy and can't give you a ride in. You'll have to make your own way to the office. Any taxi driver will know where we are. You pay for that. Have a nice evening."

"Sure. You too. Uh, thanks."

He got back into the ambulance and drove away.

The word *taciturn* had been invented to describe Simon. He'd scarcely said two words since picking me up at the airport and dropping me off here. Other than to issue orders.

Perhaps he thought a demonstration of the duties of my new job would be better than a lecture.

He was right about that.

I held out my hand to the woman. "I'm Ashley."

"Darlene. I'm the day manager. It's nice to meet you. I'll show you to your room. Do you need help with your bags?"

I had one wheelie suitcase, a backpack and a computer bag. "I can manage."

Darlene gave me a slight bow and led the way. She was an attractive woman in her early thirties. Around my age. Her smooth skin was the color of midnight.

She had sparkling white teeth and warm, friendly eyes. Her curly hair was shaved almost to the scalp on one side and tied into tight braids on the other. She wore beaded earrings that clattered like wind chimes as she moved.

My senses were overwhelmed as we walked through the grounds. I scarcely knew where to look first. The white buildings, the blue sky, the yellow sun, the purple flowers. Back home in Ontario, it was January. Filthy snow, brown slush, gray skies, black and brown clothes on scowling people.

Darlene paused when we came to a gap between the buildings. A covered patio contained tables and wicker chairs with red cushions. Lounge chairs surrounded a huge swimming pool. The white-sand beach was dotted with red umbrellas. Blue water stretched to the horizon.

"Wow," I said. "Do you ever get tired of looking at this view?"

She smiled at me. "Never. I went to university in Toronto. I got a good education. I hated every minute of it. I don't know how human beings can live in that weather. I couldn't wait to get back to the island. I hope you learn to love it as much as I do."

"I'm sure I will."

"Some don't," she said. "It can seem very confining. It's only sixty square kilometers in area. Four kilometers wide at the thickest place.

I wiped sweat off my forehead. "Is it always this hot?"

She laughed heartily. "Honey, it's winter. Just you wait till summer. Come on. You're in room 110. It's over there."

"Can I make a phone call? I told my parents I'd call them when I arrived."

"Yup, but it'll be expensive." She eyed my computer bag. "You have free Wi-Fi in your room."

"My mom doesn't trust the Internet. She thinks it still needs to have the kinks worked out."

Darlene handed me the key and left me to unpack. My accommodations were more like an apartment than a hotel room. I had one bedroom, a galley kitchen and a living room with a pull-out couch. The rooms were spacious and bright. The art and furniture were mass-produced but clean and new.

My room was on the ground floor. The private patio had white walls, a pretty iron gate and an abundance of strongly scented flowers. I dropped into one of the patio chairs and let out a long breath.

A small lizard watched me. His tail swished from side to side. His tongue flicked.

"Hi," I said. He disappeared through a crack in the wall.

*   *   *

My name is Ashley Grant. I'm thirty-three years old. I was born and raised in Prince Edward County, Ontario, and I went to college in Toronto. I'm a paramedic. I've come to the Victoria and Albert Islands on a one-year contract.

Before I left, my eldest sister, Joanne, dragged me out to get a new wardrobe for the island. She likes to shop at stores on Bloor Street in Toronto. I'd been broke before the shopping trip. After it, I was truly penniless.

I'd gone to a lot of trouble to wear the right clothes and accessories on the plane. I'd expected that Gord O'Malley, my new boss, would meet me. He hadn't. And Simon didn't seem to much care what I'd been wearing.

Simon had been waiting for me at the airport. He'd worn a uniform, so I had no trouble picking him out. We shook hands.

Then he led the way to my transportation—a bright-red ambulance. The truck wasn't even in gear when he got a call. A VSA floating off the beach by the Club Louisa Hotel. VSA means "vital signs absent." People have been known to recover after appearing to be dead, so Simon put the siren on. We sped through the streets. I hung on as everything passed in a blur of brilliant color.

Then the beach and the recovery.

Lost sandals and a ruined dress.

Nice digs though.

I closed my eyes and let the hot sun soak into my face. It felt so good.

People walked past my patio, and a woman laughed. I struggled to my feet. I had a duty to do before I got too comfortable.

I phoned home.

My mom answered so quickly, she must have been hovering by the phone. I'm the youngest of four daughters. Mom worries about me. Dad worries too, but he pretends not to.

I'm the only one of the sisters not married. I have ten nieces and nephews. You'd think that would be enough sons-in-law and grandchildren, but my mom still has hopes for me.

Heck, *I* still have hopes for me.

I shoved that thought away.

"I'm here, Mom. Safe and sound."

"That was quick," she said.

I'd landed less than two hours ago. Customs and immigration had been fast and efficient. I'd been afraid I'd have to explain to Mom what had taken so long.

"Did you remember your sunscreen? The TV says it's twenty-five degrees and sunny in Miami today."

I wasn't in Miami, and it was closer to thirty-five here. But Mom's range of experience falls between Winnipeg, Manitoba, where she grew up (cold) and Miami, Florida, where her sister lives (hot).

"Yes," I said.

"Did you meet your boss?"

"He sent a driver to pick me up. He was very nice, Mom."

"Nice?" I heard the lift in her voice. "Nice as in *nice*?"

"Nice as in older and married." Simon wore a shiny gold wedding ring. He had to be close to fifty. He was missing several teeth.

"Did you hear from John before you left?" Hope springs eternal in my mother's breast.

"No, I did not hear from John. If I had, I'd have slammed down the phone. Don't you dare forget I told you not to tell him where I've gone."

She sniffed. "I won't forget. I'm sure there are plenty of nice young men on staff for you to meet. Here's your father."

She passed the phone over.

"You've met a man already?"

"No, Dad. I was telling Mom my driver is nice."

Dad chatted on about the amount of snow that had fallen that day. The company he'd hired to plow the driveway was doing a very poor job of it.

Dad is sixty-five and overweight. He doesn't get much exercise other than clicking the TV remote and hefting beer bottles. Mom finally convinced him to hire someone to clear the snow. Needless to say, the guy concerned couldn't do the job to Dad's satisfaction. Dad had to go out and finish it properly.

I warned him about all the calls we get in winter as a result of out-of-shape men shoveling snow. He grunted. Heart attacks were things that happened to other people.

"Bye, Dad. Take care."

"Love you, honey bunch," he said.

I rummaged in my suitcase. I found a pair of shorts, a tank top and beach sandals. I went out to explore my new home.

FOUR

I ENJOYED WALKING along the gorgeous beach and exploring the hotel grounds. When I got back to my room, I unpacked and settled in. This would be my home for a year.

The salary was less than I'd earned in Ontario, but the room came with the job. It was much nicer than I'd expected.

I'd taken the job on impulse. My sisters said I was running away, and I hadn't argued with them.

I *was* running away.

I'd been a paramedic for a town on the outskirts of Toronto. I'd lived with my long-time boyfriend, John. We'd had plans to marry one day.

One night I took sick mid-shift. Nothing too serious, but I was sent home.

I found John in bed with the wife of his best friend.

I yelled and screamed. I threw things. The best friend's wife fled. John told me it was nothing. I yelled and screamed and threw more things.

I told John to get out of our house.

Unfortunately, John had bought the house before we met.

So I was the one who ended up on the street. I could have gone to my parents or to one of my sisters. But I couldn't face the humiliation. I called my best friend, Diana. Diana and I had met at work. She'd quit to take a position in the Victoria and

Albert Islands. She was due to leave in two weeks' time. I was going to miss her very much.

I arrived at her place in the middle of the night, red-eyed and weeping. She hugged me, and she took me in. She said I could stay until she left for the islands.

Diana broke her leg skiing the next day.

It was a bad break. She'd be laid up for a long time. She had to give up the new job.

We had the idea at the same time. I could take her place. We had the same qualifications.

And here I was. On Grand Victoria Island, the largest in the Victoria and Albert chain of the western Caribbean.

*   *   *

I wanted to be on my own that night, to think about all the changes in my life that had happened so quickly. I didn't want to meet with Sally at Club Louisa. But I'd said I would, so I called her. We arranged to meet for dinner at the restaurant in her hotel. I took a shower and washed the salt out of my hair. I then pulled out one of my new sundresses. Regretting the loss of the nice sandals, I slipped on a pair of colorful sneakers.

I asked Darlene how to call a cab. She did it for me. The driver gave me his card. His name was Harry. He was, according to him, the best taxi driver on the island.

The restaurant at the Club Louisa was open to the warm night air. I could hear the steady sound of surf in the distance. People laughed and chatted over drinks at the poolside bar. Candles flickered on white tablecloths. Sally had arrived before me. She jumped to her feet and squealed as I approached. She gave me a huge hug. "This is so great. Small world, eh?"

"It is nice to see you, Sally. I'm sorry about…about what happened." I took my seat.

She sat down and lifted a bottle out of the cooler on the table. "Wine?"

"Sure."

Sally filled my glass and topped up her own. It was a very expensive bottle.

"Cheers." I took a sip. Good too. I shifted in my seat, feeling awkward. Sally's father had died only hours earlier. I didn't know if she'd want to talk about him. I decided to let her take the lead.

She asked me what I'd been up to since leaving high school. I told her briefly, leaving out the part about my breakup with John. I could tell she didn't much care. Fair enough. We were just making small talk.

"I did a business degree at U of T," she said. "I help my dad with the business."

"Business?" Back in high school, Sally had been a small-town kid like me and all the others. She'd changed a lot in the past fifteen years. Her blond hair was carefully cut and colored. Her manicure and pedicure were fresh. Her dress and shoes were fashionable and expensive. An emerald ring shone on her right hand, and matching earrings were in her ears. She looked as though she'd come into money. A lot of money.

"You know my mom and dad ran a small computer shop?" she said.

I nodded.

"Dad had this really great idea for moving money around on the Internet. He sold the idea to a big company for a heck of a lot of money. I think the idea was Mom's, but she let Dad take the credit." A shadow crossed Sally's face. "Mom always did that. Anyway, he used some of the money to start up another company, and I work there."

"Where's your mother now? Did they get divorced?"

She blinked rapidly.

"I'm sorry," I said.

She glanced away. She wiped at her eyes. "Mom died five years ago. Dad took it hard. Really hard. He was lonely and sad and lost. And then *she* moved in."

"Your stepmother."

"My father's wife. Christina." Sally almost spit out the word. "They met at the opera. Of all things. One of my aunts dragged Dad to a gala opening night in Toronto. You've seen Christina. You think a woman like that would have bothered with Dad if he wasn't rich?" She took a deep drink of her wine. I said nothing.

"She married him for his money. She killed him for his money."

"That's a strong accusation, Sally," I said.

"It's true."

"Are you ready to order?" A smiling waitress stood by our table.

"No," Sally snapped.

"Can you give us a few more minutes, please?" I asked. The waitress topped up our wineglasses and left. I opened my menu. "What's good here?"

"Everything," Sally said. "I wouldn't come here if they couldn't cook. Last night I had the grilled snapper. I'm going to have it again." She shoved her unopened menu aside.

"Have you spoken to the police?" I asked.

"They sent someone around. He asked the usual questions. When we'd seen Dad last. If he'd said he was going boating. If he'd seemed depressed. Christina did her 'poor widow' act, and the cop fussed over her. Dad and I were supposed to be having breakfast together this morning. He didn't show. I told the cop that, but I don't think he cared. He was just going through the motions."

"These islands are still owned by Britain," I said. "I'm sure the police are competent."

"The cop was Canadian. Probably in a hurry to get back to the beach. I don't just *think* Christina killed my dad, Ashley. I know she did. I need you to help me prove it."

"Me? I only got here today. I don't know anyone. I haven't been anywhere other than the hospital and my hotel."

She put her wineglass down and looked at me. Her eyes were wet. "You're the only person I know here, Ashley. Other than *her*, of course."

I let out a long sigh. Now I remembered why Ashley and I hadn't been close in school. She was strong-willed and determined. When she wanted something, she wouldn't quit until she got it. Whether it was a place on the ball team, an A in history or a date with a boy. Nothing wrong with that, but it didn't make her easy to get along with. "Tell me what you think happened."

"Let's order first. Then we won't be interrupted." She waved. The waitress arrived and took our orders.

A quick look at the menu showed me prices that were way out of my range. Sally had invited me to dinner. I hoped she'd be picking up the bill. In case she wasn't, I asked for the cheapest thing they had.

Sally took a deep breath. "Dad suggested I come on this vacation. *She* didn't want me."

That seemed natural enough to me. Not many new wives would want a resentful adult child coming along on a romantic Caribbean holiday.

"She put on the loving-wife act when I was around." Sally leaned across the table. I leaned forward also.

All around us people were chatting and laughing. The surf murmured against the shore. The night breeze was light and fresh. Best of all, no mosquitoes!

"I saw her acting weird yesterday," Sally said.

"What was she doing?"

"She snuck off in the afternoon. I thought she looked shifty, so I followed. She met a guy."

"A guy? What sort of guy?"

"The sort of guy you meet when you're up to no good. She'd rented a cabana."

All the beaches on the Victoria and Albert Islands are public. Hotels put out chairs for their own guests. Earlier I'd seen some tented huts. They'd be for people who wanted complete protection from the sun. The shelters came with a door that could be closed for those who wanted privacy.

"She took one at the far end of the hotel's stretch of beach," Sally said. "She went inside. A few minutes later a man followed her. He closed the drapes behind him."

"Oh," I said.

"Yup."

"What did this guy look like?"

"Handsome. Buff. Tanned. Younger than her."

I let out a long breath. "That can't be good."

"Not for my poor dad. He was golfing. She knew he'd be gone for hours."

"Did you say anything to your father?"

Sally threw up her hands. "I wish I had, Ashley! He might still be alive."

"Has anything like that happened before?"

"I don't know for sure. My room is next door to theirs. A couple of nights ago they had a big fight. I heard them yelling at each other."

"About what?"

"I couldn't make it all out. Dad said she had to stop making a fool of herself. He threatened to divorce her."

44

"Excuse me, ladies."

I jumped. The waitress put plates on the table. She topped up Sally's wineglass again and left us.

"Your dad drowned," I said. "The ocean seemed calm enough to me. Are there bad undercurrents out there?" I hadn't seen any signs warning of unsafe waters. "Was he not a good swimmer?"

"He could swim okay. But he wasn't a keen swimmer. Dad didn't get any exercise. Other than the occasional game of golf. My mom used to nag him about that all the time." Sally smiled sadly at the memory. "Dad and I always met for breakfast at seven. Christina likes to sleep in. This morning he didn't show." Sally choked back a sob. "Dad wasn't the sort to go for a morning swim. Something, or someone, made him go out there."

She stirred the food on her plate with her fork. My vegetarian pasta looked delicious. I'd been starving when I arrived. Now I'd lost my appetite. "I'll agree that it sounds bad," I said. "But it's a long way from having an argument to killing your husband."

"Not for her."

I could think of nothing to say about that. I changed the subject. "Everything here is so beautiful. Is this your first visit to the island?"

"I came once before. A cousin of mine had her wedding here. At this hotel. It was about a year after Mom died. Dad didn't want to come, but I insisted. He was deeply depressed after we lost Mom. He needed to get away."

"He must have enjoyed it then. To want to come back."

"He had a great time. He remembered how to laugh. He looked better than he had in months."

"Good memories then."

"We both had good memories. Lots of them. *She* put an end to that."

"If you had proof, Sally, I'd tell you to talk to the police. But you don't. All you have is guesses. When are you due to go home?"

"Our flight's booked for Sunday. But we'll be staying until the police release Dad's body."

"Release the body? You mean they're going to do an autopsy?"

"The police officer told Christina that's always done when a healthy person dies with no witnesses. I bet that put a fright into her."

"Wait for the autopsy results. If your father's death was suspicious, they'll find out."

She gave me a tight smile. Her mouth had a way of turning up on one side when she smiled. "I'm glad you're here with me, Ashley." She stretched her hand across the table. I took it in mine and gave it a squeeze.

FIVE

I WOKE EARLY the next morning and went for a run on the beach. The sun was rising over the calm ocean in a cloudless blue sky. The temperature was climbing toward the thirties. It was going to be another beautiful and very hot day.

I hadn't yet bought anything to make in my own small kitchen. After my run I headed to the main hotel building for breakfast. A smiling waiter served me piping-hot coffee and fresh orange juice. I opened the menu. I swallowed. With these prices, I needed to find a grocery store—and fast.

The prevous night, Sally had signed the bill for dinner.

I read my book, drank coffee and juice and ate eggs Benedict. I planned to spend the day at the beach. I wanted to enjoy my time off. The next day I'd begin work at 7:00 AM.

When I got back to my room the little red message light on the phone was blinking. I picked it up with a sigh. Mom checking in, I expected.

Instead, Sally had left a message.

"Ashley! I've discovered something really important. Come on over. I want to show you. Meet me in my room at ten o'clock. Villa number five. Room two."

It was nine thirty now. I remembered our school days. Sally had been bossy as well as strong-willed. It seemed as though she hadn't changed.

I'd planned to put on my bathing suit and gather my beach things. Instead I picked up my purse. I found the taxi driver's card and gave him a call. He said he'd arrive at ten to ten.

I waited in the hotel lobby. The manager, Darlene, said good morning. "Going exploring?"

"I'd love to. But I have to pay a call on a friend."

She smiled. "You've made friends already. That's nice."

"Not a new friend. I ran into someone from home at Club Louisa."

Her smile faded. "Where that man died yesterday. So sad. My cousin Candice is a maid at Club Louisa. My aunt told me she was quite upset about it."

"The man's daughter is my friend."

"I am sorry to hear that. She's lucky she has you. Here's your cab now. Have a nice day, Ashley."

Harry was chatty this morning. He told me he'd lived in New York City for a few years. He hadn't liked it. He'd never been to Toronto. Did I think he'd like Toronto?

"Too cold," I said. "And it's a damp cold."

"You'll need to do some shopping soon. Best place for groceries is Food Mart. I can take you there."

"How do you know I need groceries? Can't I eat in the hotel restaurant?"

"Not with what they're payin' you down at the ambulance depot."

"How do you know…?"

"This here's the islands, Ashley. Everyone knows everything."

Only then did I realize I hadn't told him I was from Toronto. Nor had I given him my first name.

He pulled into the long driveway of the Club Louisa. "Do you know anything about the man who died here yesterday?" I asked.

Harry shrugged. "One white tourist's like another. We don't concern ourselves. That'll be ten dollars."

I handed it over. The Victoria and Albert chain of islands was a British colony, but people used American money.

The Club Louisa covered a lot of ground. The large main building was surrounded by smaller villas. I followed the signs and found number five. It was close to the swimming pools, with a great view over the ocean.

Sally opened the door of room two before I'd finished knocking.

"What's up?" I said.

She gave me a quick hug. She didn't invite me in. "Thanks for coming. Let's go."

"Go where? Tell me what you found first."

"I'd rather show you."

She led the way past the pool and down to the beach. I slipped off my shoes.

I held them in my hand as we crossed the sand. A small wooden shack stood about a hundred meters from the steps to the hotel. A green flag hung limply in the still air. The flag indicated the water conditions. Green meant safe swimming for children and for boating. Colorful paddle boats and kayaks were stacked on the sand next to the building. Several pontoon boats and a rowboat sat at water's edge. Two single-engine boats were anchored close to shore. A sailboat drifted farther out.

"I'm back," Sally called to the young man telling a couple the price of a day in the sailboat.

"Be with you in a moment, darlin'," he said. His white shorts sat low on narrow hips, and his clinging, sleeveless T-shirt did nothing to hide the muscles rippling under his dark skin. Colorful beads were woven into his long hair.

"Over here," Sally said to me. The counter of the beach shack was open to the air. Bottles of sunscreen, cheap sunglasses and straw hats filled the shelves. Flippers, masks and snorkels hung on the wall.

"You want to go snorkeling?" I said. "You didn't tell me to bring my bathing suit." Not that I'd be caught dead with my face underwater.

Bad choice of words, I reminded myself.

"Of course not," she said. "Look at this." A lined notebook lay on the counter. A pen was tied to it with a length of string. "Everything here is free to hotel guests. Except for a motorboat rental or sailboat excursion. But the equipment has to be signed out."

"Fair enough."

Sally turned the notebook around. She stabbed at a line on the paper. I peered closer. Yesterday's date was written across the top in large print. A grid of times, names, room numbers and type of equipment filled the rest of the page.

Sally stabbed at the first entry. *J. Hunt.*

"Your dad?"

"That's his room number. Villa five, suite one. Next to me."

"He took a pontoon boat out at seven thirty-five."

"So it says."

"There's nothing for the time it was returned. Do you suppose…"

"My dad was a morning person. To him, morning was a time to get work done. Even on vacation, he's in touch with the office and he wanted to get his work done before the day began. He didn't go jogging or swimming or play tennis. Not in the morning or any other time. He certainly didn't take out a boat yesterday."

"Maybe he had a reason. Maybe something was upsetting him, and he wanted some alone time on the water."

She shook her head firmly. "Not my dad."

"We'll think it over. Thanks." The couple asking about the sailboat left. The young man approached us. He gave Sally a warm smile and me a polite one.

"I brought my friend to see it," Sally said.

"Were you here when this was signed out?" I asked him.

"Can't help you, Ashley. I don't start work till nine."

"How do you know my name?"

He shrugged. "This is the islands. Everyone knows—"

"Everything. So I've been told. Has the boat been found?"

"No. It must have drifted out to sea. It'll turn up."

"Who was working here at seven yesterday?" I asked.

"Robert opens up."

"Is Robert here now?" I looked around. I didn't see anyone else.

He shook his head. The beads in his hair clinked. "I had to open myself."

"Is it usual for Robert to not come to work on time?"

The beads clattered again. "These are the islands, darlin'. We like to take things easy. But at a hotel like this one, if we take things too easy we'll be fired."

"Did he phone in sick maybe?" I asked.

"I don't have the keys. Had to call up to the boss lady to come and unlock the shack. She hadn't heard from him. She was mighty angry. It don't pay to cross her."

"I'd like to talk to Robert." Sally pulled a scrap of paper out of her pocket. "Here's my number. Can you call me when he gets here?" She handed the paper to him along, with a twenty-dollar bill.

"Sure."

Another couple arrived at the shack. He strolled over to help them.

"Interesting, don't you think?" Sally said to me.

"Robert's not coming to work today might have nothing to do with your dad."

"I don't believe that." Sally stabbed at the sign-out sheet. "Because that might be my dad's name, but it is *not* his signature."

SIX

WEDNESDAY MORNING, I jumped out of bed. I was ready and eager to start work. At ten to seven, Simon arrived in the red ambulance. We drove though quiet streets to the office. No other ambulances were in the parking area.

"Is everyone else out on call?" I asked.

Simon roared with laughter. "We're it for today. You and me. You're lucky you got me. Otherwise it'd be just you."

"Oh," I said.

We went inside. The ambulance depot consisted of one big room and a smaller one. The big room had a desk with a radio console, two cots, a couple of cheap plastic chairs and a small kitchen area. My new boss, Gord, came out of the small room, which was his office. He held out his hand and we shook. "Welcome," he said. "Fix yourself a tea or coffee if you like. Then we can start the paperwork. First, a radio and a shirt. Simon."

I'd dressed in my uniform pants from Toronto and a plain T-Shirt. Simon handed me a portable radio and a loose blue golf shirt. The shirt had the logo of the Victoria and Albert Islands on the breast pocket. The back said *Paramedic* in big white letters.

"Thanks, I..." I got no further. The radio squawked. And the day's work began.

The ambulance siren whooped and red lights flashed as we pulled out of the parking area.

"This is the only ambulance?" I said.

"Yup," Simon replied.

"What happens when it's in for service?"

"It don't get serviced."

"What? You mean never?"

"The Lord will provide." He spun the wheel as we went into a roundabout without waiting for a safe break in traffic.

I gripped the door handle. "Okay.I guess. How many other medics are on staff?"

"Three. And three drivers."

"You mean four in total? Not per shift? What happens if there are two incidents at the same time?"

"Gord helps out if he's needed."

"But there's only one ambulance."

"He has an SUV."

"Oh."

The call was to a minor accident on the highway. A car had bumped a motorbike, and the bike had gone into the ditch. The only injury was a bad cut on the motorcycle driver's arm. We took him to the hospital.

The Grand Victoria Hospital was small but well equipped. The nurse who greeted us was the one I'd met on my first day. Lucy from Scotland. "If you need anything, Ashley, just let me know. I've lived here for twenty-five years, so I'm beginning to know my way around." She laughed heartily. Other staff members came over to be introduced to the newcomer. They made me feel very welcome.

A man dressed in the blue uniform of a V&A police officer held out his hand. He gave me a broad smile. I felt myself smiling in return. He was tall and fit, with short brown hair streaked golden from the sun. He had sharp cheekbones and heavy stubble on a strong jaw. His blue eyes sparked like the ocean outside these doors. "Alan Westbrook. Pleased to meet you, Ashley. I'm from Edmonton myself."

"You're Canadian?"

"RCMP. I'm on leave from the Mounties, helping out here for a while."

"Do you like it?"

"It's a great place to live. Although the job has some challenges. As you'll find out."

Simon had told me he was going to clean the ambulance. He didn't seem to be doing much cleaning at the moment. He was in a corner, chatting to a pretty nurse. She was giggling and blushing furiously.

"Can I ask you a question?" I said to Alan.

"Sure."

"I attended at a drowning Monday."

He nodded. "I know about it. The autopsy's being done this morning. I'm here to observe."

"Are you the investigating officer?"

"I am."

"Is it possible to let me know what the results are?"

"Once I've officially notified the family, that shouldn't be a problem. Why?"

"Just curious. How difficult is it to drown someone? Deliberately, I mean."

"Not difficult at all. Not once you're in a position to hold them underwater for a few minutes."

"To do it without leaving traces, I mean. Make it look like an accident."

He let out a puff of breath. "If the victim is conscious, it's not easy. Anyone's going to struggle. Struggling leaves traces. On the victim and on the killer. Making the victim unconscious before drowning them is going to leave traces too. Do you think that happened in this case?"

"The victim's daughter suspects her father was murdered."

"Yeah, I know."

"You know?"

"I interviewed the wife and daughter. I can't tell you what was said, but accusations flew around. I gotta run. They'll start without me. Give me your phone number."

I felt heat rising into my face. He grinned at me. "So I can call you about the autopsy results."

"Oh, right. That."

*　　*　　*

The rest of the shift was quiet. I did the paperwork necessary to get paid. Gord filled me in on the details of the job. Two of the other paramedics came in to meet me, Rachel from Vancouver and Kyle from New York City. The third was on vacation.

"I'm surprised at the number of foreigners I'm meeting on the job," I said to Gord later. "Canadians like you and Alan in the police. Scottish nurses. Canadian and American medics."

"The population of this entire country is about thirty thousand."

"I've been to Blue Jays games with more people."

He laughed. "They get untold thousands of tourists here every year. They don't have enough people to do all the jobs. Luckily for them, they don't have trouble attracting people to work here."

The evening shift arrived, and I signed out. Gord gave me a lift home.

I let myself into my room. It was only three o'clock. I was looking forward to a swim and a cocktail before dinner. Dinner and an early night. I still hadn't done any grocery shopping. I also hadn't done anything about getting a cell phone to use on the island. The red message light on the phone blinked at me.

Sally. "Ashley! Call me back right away. I have to talk to you."

Thoughts of relaxation fled. I returned Sally's call.

"Where are you?" she said.

"At my place."

"What's the address? I'm coming over."

I changed out of my uniform and had a quick shower. Sally knocked on my door a few minutes later. She almost fell into the room. Her hair was mussed and her eyes wild.

"Are you okay?" I asked.

"No, I am not okay. The police have the results of my dad's autopsy."

Sally didn't take a seat. She paced across my small living room.

"Calm down," I said. "And tell me."

She whirled around. Her eyes were wide. "They found a fresh bruise on the back of Dad's head."

SEVEN

I **DROPPED** into a chair. "Wow."

"They're being all vague, of course. The cop said it could have been an accident. The paddle boat might have caught a wave and flipped. If Dad had been tossed out, he could have hit his head on a rock."

"That *is* possible, Sally."

"I showed him the paddle boat sign-out sheet. I told him that wasn't Dad's signature. I don't think he believed me."

"Why?"

"Because he doesn't want to believe that poor, sweet Christina is a ruthless killer."

"Did you speak to Sergeant Westbrook?"

"How'd you know his name?"

"I met him earlier. When I was working. I'm sure he's a competent police officer."

"Yeah, well, you weren't there when *she* put on her grieving-widow act. She has a way of twisting men around her little finger."

"Did you tell him about the man Christina met in the cabana?"

"I did. But he didn't seem to care."

"What does Christina say about all of this?"

"I don't know," Sally admitted. "He interviewed us separately. We're not exactly talking things over with each other."

"Did that guy from the boat shack ever show up?"

"No, but Westbrook says that means nothing. Sometimes islanders take off for a few days without telling anyone."

"What happens now?"

Sally threw up her hands. "Westbrook wants to keep Dad for a few more days. That means he suspects something, doesn't it?"

"I don't know, Sally."

"I'm not giving up. I know she killed my father. If you met this cop at work, that's good. You can speak to him. Tell him our suspicions. Tell him to search Christina's phone records. She might have called that guy she's having an affair with. Now that Dad's out of the way, she's probably still meeting him. Tell Westbrook to start a search for Robert, the boat attendant. Tell him—"

"Sally, I can't tell the police to do anything. You told them what you suspect. Let them take care of it."

"It might be too late, Ashley. I think she's making plans to leave."

"What do you mean?"

"The front desk clerk called my room this afternoon. She asked if I also planned to check out tomorrow. I told her she'd made a mistake. Only when I'd hung up did I wonder what she meant by *also*."

"Don't do anything foolish, Sally." I felt like I was caught in a hurricane. I needed some alone time. I didn't want to spend any more time with Sally. But I was worried she'd do something foolish. Like attack her stepmother. "Let's go for a walk on the beach. Maybe we can have a drink after."

"I'm going back to the hotel. That boat guy must have friends working there. I'm going to ask around. Try to find him. Will you come with me, please?"

"I don't..."

"I need you, Ashley. I need someone to be with me."

What could I say?

I was saved from saying anything. At that moment the phone rang.

"Sorry to bother you," Gord said. "I need you to come in to work."

"But I just got off."

"Kyle took a bad tumble on a broken patch of sidewalk. His ankle might be broken. I don't have a medic for the evening shift. You're it."

"I—"

"I told you you'll be on call when needed. You're needed now. A driver will be there in ten to pick you up."

I put down the phone.

"What's happened?" Sally said.

"I have to go to work. Sorry. Don't do anything rash, okay?"

"Me?" Sally said. "Act rashly?"

She left, and I changed back into my uniform. My phone rang just as I was locking the door behind me. I hurried inside to get it. I hoped Kyle had turned out to be okay and I wasn't needed at work.

"Is that Ashley Grant?"

73

"Speaking."

"Hi, Ashley. Alan Westbrook here. We met this morning. At the hospital. You were interested in the Julian Hunt case."

"His daughter's a friend of mine. She told me the autopsy results. He'd been hit on the head, she said. Is that what killed him?"

"The man drowned. Salt water in the lungs proves that. The autopsy did find a bruise on the back of his head. A bruise that might have been caused by a lot of things. Otherwise, no recent injuries. No signs of restraint or being in a fight. The daughter's making wild accusations. It wouldn't be wise for you to get involved, Ashley."

"I don't want to. Believe me, I don't. But Sally's angry and frightened. She has no one else."

"Here's my number," he said. "Call me if you learn anything."

I found a scrap of paper and quickly jotted it down.

"Are you seeing your friend tonight?" he asked.

"I have to go back to work. I got called in."

"Maybe I'll see you on the road then. I've pulled a double shift today too. Talk to you later." He hung up.

*   *   *

My driver tonight was a woman named Liz. She was as chatty as Simon was quiet. She spent a lot of time filling me in on the romantic complications of members of her large family. Her middle sister's youngest daughter was going with a man everyone disapproved of. I was saved from hearing why the family disapproved when we got a call.

A bar fight. Man stabbed.

Liz slapped on lights and sirens. We flew through the crowded streets of the local quarter. Away from the big hotels and condo rentals, I saw a different face of the island. Small houses, close together. Yards with carefully tended gardens or full of junk. Sometimes both on one property. People sat on their porches, enjoying the night air. Some stood in groups in the street, chatting with neighbors. Everyone stopped what they were doing to watch as we sped past.

The bar we'd been called to wasn't much more than a shack. Flashing red and blue lights in the windows advertised brands of beer. A police car was parked outside. Its lights competed with the beer advertisements.

Inside, men stood against the walls. A woman in a police uniform was talking to the onlookers. No one seemed to be under arrest. Alan Westbrook crouched beside the man on the floor.

I knelt beside him. The body lay in a pool of blood. So much blood. His throat had been slashed.

He was on his back. Empty eyes stared up at nothing. Shards of brown glass were scattered around him. A broken beer bottle. I checked for a pulse. Nothing moved under my fingers.

"Didn't have a chance," Alan said.

I glanced around the room. The police-woman was talking to the bartender.

"Killer's gone?" I asked.

"Appears so," Alan said.

"Bobby Green." Liz stood behind me.

"You know him?" Alan asked.

I got to my feet.

"He's my cousin Jeanette's youngest," she said.

"I'm sorry," I said.

"Don't be, honey. He was always up to no good."

I glanced around the bar. A couple of women sat together at a table. They were crying silently. No one else seemed partic-ularly upset. The body of Bobby Green lay in the middle of the floor. No one approached him.

"Doesn't look like he had many friends," Alan said.

"Can we take him?" I asked.

"Yeah. I've seen what I need to. Now I have to find out who."

"You won't be short of suspects, honey," Liz said. "I'll let my sister know. She can call the boy's mama."

* * *

We delivered the late Bobby Green to the morgue. We were standing outside, getting some air, when a car pulled up. Made back in the 1980s, it was now more rust than metal. A young man was driving. He jumped out, ran around the car and opened the passenger door. He helped a woman out. She wore a dress that could double as a tent. She looked at Liz. Liz looked at her.

Then the large woman and the young man went inside.

"Is that the dead man's mother?" I asked Liz. "Your cousin?"

"Yup."

"You're not friends?"

"Nope. Every family has their black sheep, honey. Bobby's mama never did him no favors. I feel sorry for the boy. He tried sometimes. Got hisself a job, I heard."

"What did he do?" I asked, although I wasn't really interested.

"Worked at one of the big fancy hotels. His mama told everyone he was the equipment manager." She snorted. "But he just checked out boats."

That got my attention. "What hotel?"

"Club Louisa. Didn't you have a call there day you arrived?"

"I did indeed. I need to make a phone call. Can I borrow yours?"

"You don't have one?"

"I haven't had time to get a local plan yet."

Liz handed me her cell phone. "I'll wait in the truck. Don't be long. My stomach tells me it's dinnertime."

I dug in my pocket for the number and made the call.

"Westbrook."

"It's Ashley Grant here. I've learned something you might want to know."

"Go ahead."

I could hear people in the background. A man shouted. Alan was probably still at the bar. Trying to find a witness who'd talk to him or his partner.

"Bobby Green worked at the Club Louisa," I said. "In the boat shack."

"Is that so?"

"Bobby. Robert. It's got to be the man who was there Monday morning. When Julian Hunt signed out a paddle boat. Or, if what my friend suspects is true, didn't sign out a paddle boat. He's the man who didn't come to work the next day."

"Thanks, Ashley."

*   *   *

At 11:00 PM I handed the night shift over to Rachel. Then I went home and fell into bed for a couple of hours' sleep. At six thirty the next morning I was up and ready for another day at work. Simon picked me up. We were on the hop most of the day.

A child stung by a jellyfish. A man who fell off the only cliff on the island and landed on the rocky beach below. The usual college-age drunks passed out on the beach before lunchtime.

Kyle, the evening-shift medic, had not broken his ankle. It was only sprained. He'd be back at work in a day or two. Gord said he'd take the extra shift today.

"Let me put in a couple of hours with Liz," I said. "You told me you like to be home when your kids get in from school. You can come back after dinner."

"Won't say no to that," my boss said. "Thanks."

As soon as he left, I spoke to Liz. "Did you hear anything more about your cousin Bobby?"

"His brothers are out lookin' for the man what killed him. Family's gathering at his mama's house."

"I'd like to pay a call on his mother."

She eyed me. "Why you wanna do that, honey?"

"To pay my condolences."

"You pay your condolences on every patient?"

"Well, no. I have some questions about him. Will you take me? I don't know where his mother lives. If we get a call, we'll leave."

She scratched her cheek. "We can't tell Gord we took the ambulance on a personal visit."

"My lips are sealed."

*   *   *

The small ramshackle house was so packed with mourners I thought it might burst at the seams. People crowded the front yard and spilled onto the street. On the way over, I'd told Liz why I was interested.

"Bobby's mama won't help you," she said. "Can't help you either. Him and his brother Jimmy were tight. Jimmy's the only one of them worth a darn. We'll talk to Jimmy."

Liz led me into the crowded house. Men smoked and drank beer in the front rooms. Women hurried in and out of the kitchen, bearing platters heaped with food.

Everyone stopped talking to stare at me. I did sort of stand out in this neighborhood. I tried to look friendly but solemn. People greeted Liz, and she greeted them in return. Some looked at her with hostility. She ignored them.

The house was hot. Too hot. The air was full of smoke and cooking smells. Too many people packed too close together.

Jimmy sat at his mother's side. He was a good-looking man in his late twenties. He wore pressed black slacks and a button-down, blue-and-white-checked shirt. He nodded to Liz.

"Jeanette," my driver said. "My condolences."

"Thank you for comin'," the large woman said. She wiped her eyes with a tissue.

"Got a minute, Jimmy?" Liz asked.

"Sure." He stood up. "Be right back, Mama."

We went outside. The mourners who'd gathered in the small yard moved aside to give us some space.

Liz introduced me to Jimmy. "Ashley's got some questions 'bout what Bobby mighta been up to."

"I'm sorry for your loss," I said.

Jimmy's dark eyes studied my face. "Thanks."

"Have the police been here? Have they asked who might have killed your brother?"

"They spoke to Mama before I arrived. To Eddie and Freddy also."

"Those two wouldn't help the police none," Liz said.

"Bobby had a job at the Club Louisa," I said. "He worked at the boat shack. Is that right?"

"Yes." Jimmy held out his hands. "My brother had some problems. All my brothers have some problems. But I keep trying. I pulled a few strings to get Bobby that job. Then the darn fool up and quit."

"Why'd he quit?"

"He said he didn't need a job anymore. More fool him. He'd come into some money. I asked him where he got it. He said he didn't steal it. He said he knew where to get more. My brothers always think they're about to come into money." His face twisted in anger.

"Did you tell the police this? It might be important."

"I didn't speak to the police."

"You didn't?"

"They didn't ask to speak to me. They won't go to a lot of trouble to find out who killed one of the Green boys. Bobby was my brother, and I loved him. But he was a lazy fool and a loudmouth. He got into an argument with a drunk in a bar.

He got himself killed." A car pulled up in front of the house, and people poured out of it. They called greetings and headed our way. "I have to go," Jimmy said. "My mother's waiting. My family's troubles have nothing to do with you, Ashley. Thanks for coming, Liz."

He went back inside.

"Get what you came for?" Liz asked me.

"I think I did."

EIGHT

WHEN I GOT HOME, I called Alan and told him what I'd learned.

"That's worth knowing, Ashley," he said. "But I don't see that it's relevant. Witnesses say a man came into the bar. He was already drunk and getting aggressive. He knocked into Bobby. Bobby spilled his beer. A fight ensued. A knife appeared. The killer ran off."

"Was this man a regular in that bar? Had he been there before?"

He sighed. "The witnesses all said they didn't know him. I could have told you that before we even questioned them."

"What do you mean?"

"That may or may not be true. It's that sort of place."

"If he was…"

"Ashley, take my advice. Don't go around asking questions. Leave it to the police. Leave it to me. This is a low-crime country, but no place is crime-free. Do you understand?"

"Yes."

"Liz Oswald gets a lot of respect on this island. They let you into Mrs. Green's because you were with her. Don't go back to that neighborhood on your own."

*   *   *

Alan thought Bobby's death had nothing to do with Julian Hunt. I didn't agree. Bobby either assigned a paddle boat to Sally's father, or he didn't. If he didn't, he knew who had wanted it to look as though he had.

He'd come into extra money.

He'd said he expected to get more.

And then he'd been killed.

Sally was right. Her father had been murdered. Perhaps even by Bobby himself. Had Bobby tried to get more money out of the person who'd hired him? Had he then been killed for his greed?

Alan had told me not to get involved.

But I was involved. Even though I didn't want to be.

By now it was very late. I went to bed. I was exhausted, but I tossed and turned most of the night. I was due to work the evening shift later that day. But instead of getting some much needed sleep, I got up with the sun.

I went for a run on the beach and then for breakfast in the restaurant. I tried to concentrate on my book, but my mind couldn't stay focused. I hadn't spoken to

Christina Hunt yet. If I wanted to find some answers, I needed to do that this morning.

Sally had told me Christina was planning to leave the island today. I'd forgotten to ask Alan if he knew about that.

He'd told me not to be asking questions. I figured he meant asking questions in the Greens' neighborhood. Not at Club Louisa.

I arrived at Club Louisa shortly after ten. I didn't know what I thought I could do there. I was no detective. I couldn't accuse Christina outright of hiring a hit man. Two hit men, if the greedy Bobby had been taken care of too.

I'd speak to Christina on the pretext of offering my condolences. I'd take it from there. If Christina wasn't around, I'd look for Sally. Sally had said she was going to ask the hotel staff about Robert.

It was highly unlikely any of them would talk to her. She might not have heard that Robert, aka Bobby, had been killed.

The cab dropped me off in front of the hotel's main building. I didn't go inside but headed for the neat white villa in which the Hunts were staying.

My hotel was nice, but the Club Louisa took it up a notch. Maybe two notches.

It was quiet. Not many guests were around. A gardener trimmed a hedge, while another deadheaded flowers. A maid pushed a loaded housekeeping cart. A light, refreshing wind stirred the palm trees. The ocean sparkled in the sun. Alan had told me this was a low-crime country. It didn't have the sort of security I'd seen in other Caribbean destinations. No gates, no guards. I simply walked around.

Villa five, where Sally had her room, was one of the last on the property. Four rooms were on the main level of the villa.

Three of the doors were closed. A house-keeping cart sat in the corridor. A maid came out of the open door across from Sally's room. She nodded politely to me. She was young, short and thin. Her skin was a deep black. She had large dark eyes and a pretty, heart-shaped face.

I said, "Good morning."

"Morning." She took a pile of fluffy white towels off the cart. She looked a lot like Darlene, the manager of my hotel. I stopped abruptly. A name tag was attached to her hotel uniform. Candice.

"You wouldn't be related to Darlene, who works at the Ocean Breeze, would you?"

Her smile lit up her face. "Sure would be. You know Darlene?"

"Yes, I do." I held out my hand. "I'm Ashley."

"The new medic? Welcome." We shook hands.

"I'm here to pay a call on Christina Hunt. Is that her room?" I pointed.

"Yes, but she's not in right now. She went out about fifteen minutes ago. Poor lady."

"You mean because her husband died?"

Candice's bright smile faded. Her eyes filled with tears. "It's so sad. He was such a nice man. She's a lovely lady." She fumbled in her pocket for a tissue.

"You met them?"

"Yes. Some of the guests here are bossy and rude. Some are very nice. She's very nice. She leaves a good tip every day. I don't mean she's nice because of the tip. But it shows her character."

"What about him? Mr. Hunt?"

The tears were flowing heavily now.

"Gosh, I'm sorry," I said. "I don't mean to upset you."

She blew her nose. "It's fine. He was… he was great. A nice man."

She stuffed the tissue back into her pocket. She grabbed a pile of towels and held them to her chest. "I'm sorry. I have work to do."

"Okay. Nice meeting you."

"If you're looking for Mrs. Hunt, she had her swimming costume on. She might be by the pool."

"Thanks. What time's checkout?"

"Noon."

"Are Mrs. Hunt and Sally Hunt leaving today?"

"No. I would have been told."

I found Christina doing laps in the infinity pool. Her swimming stroke was strong and powerful. Families and children played in the larger pool, but Christina had this one to herself. I took a seat on a lounge chair next to a small table holding a book and sunglasses. A hotel towel and a big straw hat were tossed onto the chair on the other side of the table. I recognized the blue-and-gold wrap. Christina had been wearing it the day her husband died.

I leaned back in the chair and closed my eyes. This, I thought, was the life. The sun was hot on my bare legs and arms. I go from pasty white to sunburned without getting a tan in between. But I'd be okay in the sun for a couple of minutes while waiting for Christina.

*   *   *

Drops of cool water splashed on my legs. I woke with a start. A dark shape loomed over me. I quickly sat up and swung my legs off the chair.

"Be careful," the woman said. "You can get a bad burn sleeping in the sun." She grabbed the towel and wrapped it around her slim body. Even without makeup and with her dark blond hair wet, she was beautiful. The delicate skin beneath her eyes was dark and puffy. Fine lines radiated out from the corners of her mouth.

She slipped her sunglasses on. "I recognize you. You were here the other day and at the hospital. You helped...you tried to help my husband."

"I'm Ashley Grant. I'm a paramedic with the V&A health service."

"Do you have news about my husband's...body?" She shook her head before I could answer. "No. If there were news, it would be delivered by someone in more official clothes."

I wore shorts and a Toronto Blue Jays T-shirt. I flushed. "Sorry. That's not why I'm here. I'm a friend of Sally's. That is, I knew her when we were in school."

I couldn't see Christina's eyes through her Ralph Lauren sunglasses. But I felt them study me. "My stepdaughter is having a very difficult time dealing with her father's death."

"Yes, I know."

"She might have told you that I killed him."

"She—"

"I assure you, I did not. Nor did I want to." She let out a long sigh. She dropped into her chair. "Sally and I have never gotten on. She expected her father to mourn her mother for the rest of his life. She couldn't accept that he could find happiness again. With me. And we were very happy. In the short time we had." She took off her sunglasses and stared up at me. Her eyes were wet. "If you have nothing to tell me, please leave me in peace."

"Sorry," I mumbled. I fled.

Hurrying toward the villas, I spotted Candice, the maid I'd spoken to earlier. She stood in a doorway, watching me. She did not smile.

NINE

I DIDN'T HEAR from Sally for two days. My time was taken up with working, which included extra shifts to cover the injured Kyle, and getting to know my new island home. Harry, the cab driver, ferried me around. Liz, the afternoon-shift driver, filled me in on all the best places to shop. Lucy from the hospital invited me to dinner with her and some of her friends. I got an island phone plan. I put the handful of local numbers I had into my contacts list.

I didn't hear from Alan Westbrook. I told myself I wasn't disappointed. I only wanted to know what was happening with the case.

I did hear from my parents. Every night. Mom worried that I was getting too much sun. She worried that the food wasn't agreeing with me. She asked if I'd met any eligible young men yet. (*Too busy*, I replied). Dad worried about me living on my own in a foreign country.

I worked night shift on Saturday. Kyle returned to work. That meant I would have all day Sunday off.

I was yawning heavily when I got out of the cab just after nine on Sunday morning. We'd had a last-minute call to a serious car accident, and I was late getting home.

Darlene came out of the office. She gave me a wave. People here usually dress very nicely. Today the hotel manager was in a pretty blue dress tied by a thick white belt. Her blue shoes had high heels.

A small white hat sat on her head. A woman and a child were with her. The woman was Darlene's cousin, Candice. She held the child's hand. The little girl wore a frothy pink dress and pink socks trimmed with white lace. A mass of pink ribbons had been wound into her curly hair.

"Good morning," Darlene said. "You're home late, Ashley. Busy night?"

"It was. Are you working today? On Sunday?" Most businesses on the island close on Sundays.

She shook her head. "I forgot something. We're on our way to church, so we stopped by. This is my cousin, Candice."

"We've met. Hi again."

"Good morning," Candice said.

The little girl gave me a huge smile.

"And what's your name?" I asked.

"Rose. I'm almost four."

"What a beautiful name." Rose's skin was the color of coffee with a lot of cream added.

I couldn't help but glance at the cousins, both of them deep black.

"Have you heard if anything's happening about Julian Hunt's death?" I asked Candice.

Her lovely eyes clouded over. "No. Mrs. Hunt and her stepdaughter are due to leave today. I don't know if they will be." I glanced again at the smiling child. I saw something familiar in the tilt of her mouth.

"Have you worked at the Club Louisa for long?" I asked Candice.

"Six years." She stared at me.

"I'm sorry for your loss," I said.

Candice's eyes opened wide in surprise. I gave her a small nod. She lowered her head and whispered, "Thank you."

"We have to go," Darlene said, "or we'll be late."

They got into a Toyota Corolla parked by the office doors. The car was clean and rust-free, about five years old.

Darlene fastened Rose into the backseat. Candice got behind the wheel. Rose waved as they drove away. The car windows were down. The child's pink ribbons blew around her head. I waved back.

In my room, I took off my uniform and had a quick shower. I put on my pajamas and crawled into bed. I'm used to sleeping in the daytime, but today I couldn't fall asleep. I lay in bed for a long time, looking up at ceiling. The room phone rang. I hurried to answer it.

"Hi, Ashley." Sally. "I'm calling to say bye. Keep in touch, will you?"

"You're leaving?"

"The police released Dad's body last night. No reason to hang around, is there?"

"Did anything happen with your suspicions?"

"Stupid cops. I told them to investigate Christina, but they wouldn't. Tell you the truth, Ashley, I think that guy in charge is incompetent. I bet the Mounties sent him down here to get him out of the way."

"You mean Sergeant Westbrook?"

"Yeah, that one. He might be cute, but he's as dumb as a stack of bricks."

"The police aren't going to tell you details of their investigation, Sally. Maybe they looked and didn't find anything."

She snorted. "I'm not dropping this, you know. When we get back to Canada, I'm going to insist on talking to someone. Someone important. She killed my dad. She's not going to get away with it."

"What time's your flight?"

"Six."

"How about I come around now? I'd like to say goodbye in person."

"If you want," she said. "I'll be here."

My next call was to Alan Westbrook.

"I know it's none of my business," I said when he answered, "but has anything happened with the Bobby Green murder?"

"Good morning to you too, Ashley. Lovely day, isn't it?"

"I'm sorry." I let out a breath. "I might have a lead, that's all."

"Not a problem. I'll go first. Bobby Green seems to have come into some money all of a sudden. Stupidly, he was flashing it around. The night he died, he treated the entire bar to a round. He was a small-time crook, but not a very smart one. His brothers are different. They play in what passes for the big leagues on the islands. Meaning drug smuggling. I've heard rumors of human trafficking. They're in way over their heads and have some powerful enemies. Officially, we think whoever killed Bobby did it as a warning to Edward and Fredrick. One witness gave us a rough description of the man running out of the bar. If it's who we think it is, he was on the first flight to Miami the next morning. The witness wasn't located for more than twelve hours. We were too late. The flight had landed, and he'd disappeared. The Miami police have been notified."

"You say *officially*. Is that what you think happened? A falling out among bad guys?"

He hesitated. "I have no reason to think otherwise."

"Well, I do. I think someone took Julian Hunt out on a paddle boat on Monday morning. They hit him over the head and pushed him into the water to drown. I think they bribed Robert, aka Bobby, to lie about the boat. Robert came back for more money. Julian's killer realized she had to get rid of him. Permanently."

"You say she?"

"Christina Hunt."

"Why would Mrs. Hunt do this?"

"Money. Maybe she was cheating and her rich husband was threatening to divorce her."

"This is too much to talk about on the phone, Ashley. Where are you?"

"I'm at my place. I'm going to Club Louisa. Sally and Christina are leaving today. If I'm going to talk to them, it has to be now." I glanced at the clock on the wall. It was almost eleven. Checkout time was noon.

"You might be onto something. But you have to let us handle it, Ashley."

"I've told Sally I'm coming around to say goodbye. I might be able to get Christina to talk, whereas you can't."

"Ashley." A warning was in his voice.

"Let me do this, Alan."

He sighed and gave in. "I'll meet you there. I'm on the other side of the island. I'll be at least half an hour. Don't do anything without me."

*   *   *

Harry picked me up within minutes of my call. He was, he said, just passing by. I arrived at Club Louisa ten minutes after hanging up on Alan. I paced up and down in front of the main doors. The lobby was crowded with people checking out.

I decided not to wait for Alan to arrive. I headed for villa five.

Sally opened the door to my knock. The corner of her mouth turned up in her crooked smile. She wrapped me in a hug. "Nice of you to come and say goodbye."

I glanced behind her. A suitcase lay open on the bed among a jumble of clothes, shoes and jewelry.

"I've learned something that might be important," I said.

"About my dad? Come on in."

"I'd like to talk to Christina too. Is she in her room?"

Sally's eyes darkened. "I have absolutely no idea where she is. Probably having one last meeting with her secret lover."

"I'll check," I said. "Wait here."

Christina answered my knock. She was dressed for traveling, in loose blue pants and a white shirt. She wore a thin gold necklace and small gold earrings. Her two suitcases sat by the door.

"I'm Ashley. Remember me?"

"I do." Her voice was cool. "I'm sorry, but I'm leaving shortly for the airport." She made no move to invite me in.

"That's okay. I have something I want to talk to you about. You and Sally." I gestured down the hall. "Together."

"I doubt that my stepdaughter wants to talk to me. She's made that plain."

"Won't take long," I said.

"Very well." Christina reached behind her and grabbed the room key off a side table. She stepped into the corridor. The door to her room closed silently behind her.

Sally was sitting on her bed, arms crossed over her chest. She glared at Christina.

Christina's face softened. "Sally, dear, I don't want us to…"

"I am not your *dear*," Sally snapped. "Get on with it, Ashley. I haven't got all day here."

I glanced from one woman to the other. Now that I was here, I wasn't so sure of my facts after all. Alan had told me not to get involved. Was I being fanciful? Had Julian taken out a boat alone and had an accident? Had Bobby simply fallen afoul of some bad people?

I took a deep breath. "Did you know that Julian fathered a child when he was here four years ago?"

Sally sucked in a breath. Christina's eyes widened.

"I don't see that that's any of your business." Christina's voice was cool.

"You can't go around saying that," Sally said.

"Neither of you seems surprised," I said. "I met the little girl. Her name's Rose, and she's gorgeous. She doesn't look like Julian. But she does look a lot like you, Sally. You have the same slightly crooked smile."

"I don't know why you're doing this." Sally stood up. There was no trace of the smile now. "But you can get out of here."

"I'm doing this because you asked me to, Sally. You got me involved in your father's murder."

"It was an accident," Christina said. "A sad, tragic, horrible accident. You have to let it go, Sally."

"I'll never let it go," Sally said. "Not until I see you in jail. Where you belong."

Christina just shook her head.

"Was it a shock to him?" I asked. "To come back here and see the maid he'd had a holiday fling with? To be told he had a daughter?"

"No," Christina said. "He knew about Rose. Julian was a good man. He did the right thing and had been sending money for the child since her birth. He told me before we married, but not any of the details. Which is why I foolishly booked a vacation on this island and at this very hotel. Sally once mentioned that he'd enjoyed this place the last time he was here."

"He'd been tricked by a nasty, greedy woman," Sally yelled. "That child's not my father's. If there even is a child."

"I've met her. She's very sweet," I said. "The mother's still working here as a maid. She's not making a living out of fleecing rich, lonely men. Your dad was sending her just enough for her to put some money away for the child's education. To buy a few nice things to help her out." Like a used car. "I believe she genuinely cared for him. She was probably happy to see him again. She was very upset when he died."

"Of course she was," Sally said. "She was sad when his bank account died, not him."

"Is that why you killed him?" I asked. "So he wouldn't send her any more money?"

"I didn't—" Christina said.

"Not you, Christina. But you, Sally. You didn't know about this child, did you? Must have been a heck of a surprise to you when he told you. Did he actually introduce you to the woman?"

"No," Christina said. "It was me who introduced them. I thought she was charming. I told her I was pleased to meet her. She said she was delighted that Julian had found happiness again. I suggested we go to their house and meet the child. But Julian said no. He didn't want to be involved in their lives."

"He always was a sucker," Sally said.

"Did you plan to kill him?" I asked her. "Or did that just happen?"

"This conversation is over. Get out, both of you." Sally's eyes had narrowed in anger. A vein pulsed in her neck.

I'd been such a fool.

I pulled out my phone.

"What are you doing?" Sally asked.

"Phoning the police, of course. Sergeant Westbrook told me they've found the paddle boat." He had, of course, not said any such thing. "They're checking it for fingerprints today."

"They can't…"

"Can't what, Sally? Can't have found it? The waters around this island are very shallow. You have to get past the reef to reach ocean depths. Didn't you realize that when you sunk it?"

She jumped off the bed and grabbed the phone out of my hand.

"Sally!" Christina yelled.

I lunged for my phone. Sally threw it across the room. Then she kicked me. Hard. She'd been aiming for my right knee, but I turned just in time. The blow hit me on the side of the leg, and I went down.

Christina ran toward Sally. Sally grabbed her computer bag off the side table. She swung it at Christina's head. I heard it connect, and Christina fell onto the bed with a cry.

Sally ran out the door.

TEN

I **PUSHED MYSELF** to my feet. My leg hurt, but nothing seemed to be broken. I ran to help Christina. She groaned and struggled to sit up.

"Are you okay?" I asked.

"Yes. I think so."

"Don't try to get up." I examined her hairline. She'd have a mighty big bruise the next day and a headache to match. But the bag had not broken the skin. "Stay still. I'm a medic. Let me look."

"No. No time. I'm fine. We have to go after her."

She struggled to stand. I gave in and helped her to her feet. She swayed but remained upright.

My phone had hit the wall. It lay on the floor beside the verandah doors. I scooped it up and pushed buttons. It was still working. "I'm phoning the police."

Christina ran out the door. I followed, punching in Alan Westbrook's number as I ran.

"Sally killed her dad," I gasped. "She confessed to it. She attacked me and Christina. She's running away. We're at Club Louisa. I'm after her."

"No!" Alan said. "Keep back. I'm almost there."

Christina ran across the pool deck. Sally was well ahead of her, flying down the boardwalk to the beach.

"She's heading for the boat shack. She's going to get away!" I yelled.

"Stay where you are. I'm sending a police boat."

"I can't. Christina needs help." I shoved the phone into my pocket and ran.

Startled guests and hotel staff watched us pass.

I hit the beach. I kept running. Sally was well ahead of us. Her feet were bare. I wore running shoes, a disadvantage in the soft sand.

She reached the boat shack. The man staffing the shack was helping a family put on life jackets. Sally leaned over the counter and came up with something in her hands. Keys. Two motorboats bobbed in the calm water about thirty meters offshore.

Sally waded in up to her waist. Then she dove into the water and swam. She reached the closest boat. She grabbed the ladder draped over its side and scrambled aboard.

The hotel employee realized what was going on. He yelled and waved his arms.

Sally's boat started with a roar. She spun the wheel and headed for the open ocean.

"Hey! You can't take that out!" the man shouted.

Christina stood up to her knees in the water. She turned to the man as I ran up. "We have to go after her. She's not in her right mind. Give me the keys for the other boat."

He hesitated.

"The police are coming," I said. "If we can follow her, we can tell them where to go."

"Okay, but I'm driving."

He ran to the shack and grabbed the keys. By the time he got to the boat, Christina and I were already in it. Christina pulled up the anchor.

"That boat's bigger than this one," he said. The engine started with a roar.

"Then you'd better be a good pilot," Christina answered.

"Does Sally know boats?" I asked.

"Oh yes," Christina said. "I have a cottage on Lake Muskoka. I let her use my boat whenever she wants."

"Different on the ocean," the man said. "Very different. I'm Jeremy. I don't think we've been properly introduced."

Christina laughed. "No time like the present."

Our boat bounded over the waves. The wind tore at my hair.

Christina's laugh died, and she turned to me. "I tried so hard to get her to like me. But everything I did seemed to make things worse. She never accepted my marriage to her father. I tried to understand. I thought she hated me because I encouraged him to get on with his life after her mother died."

"Instead," I said, "she hated *him* for it." My hair whipped around my face. Salt spray stung my eyes. We were keeping pace with the other boat but not gaining. Sally stood at the wheel. She did not look back.

"I think," Christina said, "she's just a hater."

Jeremy pulled out his phone. He held it with one hand and controlled the steering wheel with his other. "We're off Cape Sophia. She's heading due north. Blue-and-white boat with red trim. I'm about two hundred meters behind. Got it."

He hung up. "The police boat's almost here. We don't have a lot of gas. But I filled the other one up last night."

"Keep going," Christina ordered.

Our boat began to slow down.

"What are you doing?" she yelled. "We have to keep up with her."

"She doesn't know these waters," Jeremy said. "She's heading straight for the reef."

Ahead, a line of white water marked where waves broke on the rocks. To our right a handful of charter boats bobbed in the sea. People were in the water, snorkelers and divers exploring the rich life of the reef.

Sally had seen the danger. Her boat slowed and turned left. Then it sped up again. It ran beside the rough waters of the reef.

"She knows she's going too fast to try to find a path through," Jeremy said. Our boat also sped up. He took his hand off the wheel and pointed. "There. Look. Police boat."

A large blue-and-white launch was heading for Sally. The flag of the V&A fluttered from the stern. Men and women in uniform stood on the deck.

Sally saw them too. Once more her boat turned north, out to the open ocean.

"Don't do it," Jeremy muttered. Our boat slowed to a halt. Christina gripped the railing. Her knuckles had turned pure white.

Sally's boat passed into the line of breaking waves. It rose on the swell of water and then plunged down. I heard the sound of metal tearing. It lurched forward again but began tilting to one side. It slowed and then came to a shuddering stop. The engine screamed as Sally tried to force it to keep moving. She whirled around and stared over the churning water at me. We were close enough that I could see her eyes. They were wild, frightened and furious. She had torn the bottom out of her boat.

The large police boat stopped short of the reef. It launched a dinghy with two officers in it. "Police," a voice yelled through a loudspeaker. "Prepare to be boarded. Put your hands up."

Sally climbed onto the gunnel. She stared down into the churning water.

"Please, no," Christina whispered.

"She'll cut herself to ribbons if she tries to swim," Jeremy said.

The police dinghy pulled up beside her.

Sally turned. Again she looked directly at me.

Then she stepped down, back into the boat. An officer scrambled aboard after her.

I let out a long sigh of relief. Christina dropped into a chair with a sob. She buried her head in her hands.

"Good one," Jeremy said. "Anytime you ladies want to do that again, I'm your man."

Only then did I realize where I was. On the open ocean. And what I was standing in. A small boat. I swallowed.

"You okay?" Jeremy said. "You're not going to be sick, are you?"

I looked back the way we'd come. The turquoise water, the line of white sand, the big beautiful hotels, the clear blue sky.

"No," I said. "I'm not going to be sick. In fact, I think I'm going to be just fine."

ELEVEN

SALLY, HANDS CUFFED behind her back, was helped onto the launch. One of the officers tied a rope to the boat she had stolen so it could be pulled off the reef by the police launch. Jeremy, Christina and I followed it to the police dock.

"That was exciting," Jeremy said to me. "What's the story?"

"You'll be reading all about it in the papers." I went to stand beside Christina. I slipped my arm around her shoulders. Her body shivered. Tears ran down her face.

Alan Westbrook stood on the dock, waiting for us. He watched as Sally was escorted off the police boat. He spoke to the officers and pointed toward a waiting patrol car. Two officers marched Sally toward it. She didn't turn around.

Christina and I clambered out of our boat. Jeremy threw a rope onto the dock.

Alan approached us. "You all okay?"

"I'm good," I said. I was more than good. I'd been on a small boat on the open ocean and I'd survived. I'd probably come down with an attack of nerves later, but right now I was perfectly calm.

"I'll arrange for a ride back to your hotel, Mrs. Hunt," he said.

"No," Christina said. "I want to go with Sally."

"I don't think she wants you to," I said.

The patrol car drove away. It did not put on lights and sirens.

"That doesn't matter," Christina said. "She's Julian's daughter. She's my responsibility now. Do you know any good lawyers, Sergeant?"

"I can give you a number. Do you want to come to the station with me?"

Christina nodded.

"Janet!" he called to a policewoman. "Please show Mrs. Hunt to my car. I'll be with you in a moment."

"Come with me, madam," Janet said.

When they'd walked away, Alan turned to me. "Do you need a lift home, Ashley?"

"I can find my way, thanks. I need to go back to the Club Louisa for my bag." I eyed Jeremy and the motorboat. "I might even hitch a ride on that boat." I let out a long breath. "I was played for a sucker, wasn't I?"

Alan grinned at me. "I'd say you led us to a successful conclusion."

"What happens now?"

"Sally will be charged with the murder of Julian Hunt and with attempting to escape arrest. That will be for starters. You'll be called as a witness. Christina also, although I have a feeling she won't want to testify."

"I'm not going anywhere," I said.

"Good." He smiled at me. "I mean that in more ways than one. I have to go now. Can I take you out to dinner later? I can fill you in on what's happened."

"Sure. I'd like that." I returned his smile.

TWELVE

THE SUN WAS DIPPING behind the hills to the west when Alan picked me up. We went to a place on the beach. The restaurant seemed to be made of nothing but wood planks and rope. Lanterns had been hung from the rafters and placed along the railing. In the open kitchen, men chopped vegetables and stirred huge pots. People laughed, and reggae music played softly. We were shown to a picnic table on the sand. Alan had a beer, and I ordered a rum cocktail.

"You were quick to guess that Candice's child was Julian's," Alan said. The waiter brought our drinks, and we clinked glasses.

"It was much more than the color of Rose's skin," I said. "She made me think of Sally in one very important way— how her lip turned up when she smiled. In other circumstances, I might not have realized what it meant. But when I talked to Candice at the hotel, she seemed to be truly grieving for Julian. More than because he was a nice guest. When I saw Rose, I knew why."

"That was smart."

"Not really. I studied biology at university. I'd planned to be a medical researcher until the medic bug bit me. My interest was in genetic inheritance. Everything we have, we get from our parents. Our looks. Our health. Our habits and our mannerisms."

"Not everything, I hope," he said.

"No it sounds as though Sally's parents were both nice people. Julian didn't want to be involved with the child he'd fathered, but he did want to do right by her."

Alan sipped his beer.

"Does Sally have anything to say?" I asked.

"Not much, but enough that I can piece together what happened. Her father told her he'd decided to include little Rose in his will. Sally didn't care for that. First a wife, and now a sister to share her inheritance with. He'd had a heart attack a year ago, and his overall health wasn't good. Sally decided to get rid of him before he got home and rewrote the will."

"And she convinced me to help her point the guilt at Christina. She must have been laughing at poor gullible me all the time."

"Don't be too hard on yourself, Ashley. It's tough to believe someone we know is capable of something like that."

I still felt like a fool. Everything Sally had said to me, I'd believed without question.

"Even if she'd gotten away with it," Alan said, "it would have been for nothing. Julian didn't have much money."

"I thought he was rich."

"So did Sally. He made a lot of money when he and Sally's mother sold their first company. He lost almost all of it through some bad investments."

"The Club Louisa can't be cheap," I said.

He grinned. "It isn't. Christina paid for the holiday. Christina is a wealthy woman in her own right."

"What?"

"That's right. Which is why I never took Sally's accusations seriously. I'd checked

Christina's and Julian's bank accounts.
I knew Christina wouldn't have killed him
for money. No one would have killed him,
I thought, for money. I didn't realize Sally
didn't know about it. Christina, by the way,
intends to continue sending the monthly
allowance to Candice for the care of Rose."

"That's nice of her."

"It's not a lot, but it will help with
Rose's future."

"Sally told me Christina was seeing some
guy at the hotel. I'm guessing that was a lie."

"First I've heard of it. If it had been
true, Sally would have used it to focus my
attention on Christina."

"What actually happened, do you
think?"

"Sally says it was an accident. She and
her dad went for a pre-breakfast ride in
a paddle boat. They had a mishap. The
boat sunk. Julian died. She decided to pin
the death on Christina. She says she only

wanted to scare the woman. She didn't intend to have Christina charged with Julian's murder."

"Another lie."

"We found the paddle boat, by the way. It was in a rocky cove in about three meters of water. Giant hole in the bottom."

"What about the signature on the sign-out sheet? What about Robert?"

"The signature was Julian's. No doubt about it." Alan eyed me. "Which is why people who don't have police resources shouldn't interfere in police investigations."

"How did Sally get back to the hotel?"

"I suspect she hailed an illegal cab to take her back to the hotel. Even if we'd asked anyone who might have seen her to get in touch with us, a jitney driver wouldn't."

I sipped my drink.

"Sally paid Robert off. Told him to say Julian had gone out with Christina. What she didn't realize was that Bobby Green was not only greedy, but he also wasn't too smart. He took her money. Then he came back for more."

"You think she had him killed?"

"I do."

"How would she do that? How would someone even go about finding a hit man?"

"Consider yourself lucky you don't know, Ashley. We're starting to get some police records from Canada. Sally was no angel. She's never been charged with anything, but she is definitely on police radar."

"Haven't I been a fool," I said.

"Are you ready to order?" the waiter asked.

"I haven't even looked at the menu yet," I said. "Give me a couple of minutes?"

"No problem."

"The fish tacos are great," Alan said.

My phone rang. "Probably my mother," I said.

It rang again.

"Go ahead and answer," Alan said. "We have to keep our mothers happy."

"Ashley! We need you."

"What? Who needs me? Why? Who is this?"

"Liz, of course. Kyle had a giant fight with his boyfriend. He quit. He's leaving the island. Tonight."

"Can he do that?"

"No, he can't do that. But he has. I'm not working this shift alone."

"What about Rachel or Gord?" I said.

"Gord's wife's gallery is having their big reception tonight. The governor himself is going to be there. He'll kill me if I call him. Rachel isn't answering."

"But...but..."

"That's the radio now. Multi-car accident on the highway. I'll swing by your hotel."

"I'm not there, I'm..."

Alan stood up. He threw money on the table. "Tell Liz you'll meet her at the scene. I'll drop you."

We ran for his car.

I settled myself into the passenger seat and did up my seat belt.

I glanced at the man beside me. He turned his head and gave me a grin. Then he put the car into gear.

Life on the Victoria and Albert Islands was going to be very interesting indeed.

VICKI DELANY is one of Canada's most prolific and varied crime writers. She is the author of more than twenty-five crime novels, including standalone Gothic thrillers, the Constable Molly Smith series, the Klondike Gold Rush Mysteries and the Year Round Christmas Mysteries. Under the pen name of Eva Gates, she is the national bestselling author of the Lighthouse Library cozy series.

The first book in her Sergeant Ray Robertson series for Rapid Reads, *Juba Good*, was nominated for a Derringer Award, an Arthur Ellis Award and the Ontario Library Association's Golden Oak Award.

Vicki lives in Prince Edward County, Ontario. She is the past president of the Crime Writers of Canada. For more information visit www.vickidelany.com.